Bedtime!

BY **Joan Blos**

ILLUSTRATED BY **Stephen Lambert**

Simon & Schuster Books for Young Readers

SIMON & SCHUSTER BOOKS FOR YOUNG READERS
An imprint of Simon & Schuster Children's Publishing Division
1230 Avenue of the Americas, New York, New York 10020

Book design by Anahid Hamparian
The text for this book is set in 20-point Dutch 809.
The illustrations are rendered in chalk pastels.
Printed and bound in Hong Kong by South China Printing Co.(1988) Ltd.
First Edition
10 9 8 7 6 5 4 3 2 1
Library of Congress Cataloging-in-Publication Data
Blos, Joan W. Bedtime! / by Joan W. Blos; illustrated by Stephen Lambert.—
p.   cm.
Summary: After his grandmother has tucked his stuffed animals into bed one by one, a young boy is ready to go to sleep himself.
ISBN 0-689-81031-8 (hc)
[1. Bedtime—Fiction. 2. Grandmothers—Fiction. 3. Toys—Fiction.]
I. Lambert, Stephen, 1964– ill. II. Title.
PZ7.B6237Be 1998
[E]—dc20 96-42100

To Nico, Steiner,
Tarbear & Little
—J.B.

The clock said it.

The darkness outside said it.

And the grandma said it, "Bedtime!"

But the little boy said, "No."

The little boy was playing
with his 1-2-3 fur friends.
The friends were Bear, and Clown
(who was really a monkey
dressed like a clown), and Tiger.

After a while the little boy said, "I'm not sleepy, and Tiger and Clown aren't sleepy.
But maybe Bear is sleepy."

So do you know what that grandma did?
She took that sleepy Bear and she put him into the bed.
Then she pulled up the covers and gave him a kiss.
And she said to him, "Good night, Bear."

It wasn't long before the little boy said, "I'm not tired, and Clown isn't tired. But maybe Tiger is tired."

So do you know what that grandma did?
She took that tired Tiger and she put him
into the bed. Then she pulled up the covers
and gave him a kiss. And she said to him,
"Good night, Tiger."

Then Clown was all alone and the little boy
said to his grandma, "I think Clown is lonely!"

So do you know what that grandma did? She took that lonely Clown and she put him into the bed. She put him next to Tiger who was next to Bear. She pulled up the covers and gave him a kiss. And she said to him, "Good night, Clown."

When Bear and Tiger
were all tucked in,
and Clown was tucked in too,
the grandma sat down
in the rocking chair
with no one sitting on her lap
and began to read a story
to Bear and Tiger and Clown.

After a while the little boy stopped playing
the game that he was playing
and the grandma lifted him onto her lap
and they finished the story together.

So now it was *really* bedtime!
The clock said it,
   the darkness said it
      the grandma said it—

and the little boy said it, too!

He was even ready to put his pajamas on.

Then he got right into his nice safe bed
with Bear and Tiger and Clown.
And the grandma pulled up the covers
and gave him a good-night kiss.

And when she said, "Good night,
little boy!" he almost didn't hear her.
That's how fast he fell asleep!